Three Stories About
'Awkward Moments Bloom'

Featuring the Poplar Family
learning the language of Focusing.

Written by Sandy Jahmi Burg
Illustrated by Molly Guterriez, Nomi Miller &
Sarah Johnson

Smartview Stories™

First Published in USA in 2021
by Smartview Stories
www.smartviewstories.com

Editor: Inge Smith Terrill
Map Design: Renee La Roi
Graphic Design: Renee La Roi

Book 1
Flesch-Kincaid Reading Levels
Three Stories: Grade 3
Supplemental Pages: Grades 4-6
The characters and events portrayed in this
book are fictitious and based on real life
experiences. There is an understanding
that human beings are living processes.

9 781737 632405

**Smartview Stories is a children's self-empowerment book project for ages 9-99.
That is, for the child within us all.**

You might be attracted to this series IF:

You are curious and like to read book series.

You would like a new perspective on what it is like to be human.

You teach emotional literacy and want to share this with students.

You are wanting to improve your relational skills with yourself, others or your environment.

You are interested in community living, permaculture, or sustainable living concepts.

You are interested in learning Focusing skills.

You like to geek out on neuroscience.

You have a fondness for visiting Floyd, VA.

Dedication

Smartview Stories honor the creative potential within each of us yearning to be expressed.

Cheers!

It's a lusciously
ripe time to adventure
as a human being.

Enjoy being YOU! ♡

Sandy Jahmi Burg

4

Table of Contents

Foreword

No one teaches us how to live in a body. Wouldn't it be helpful to know the best way to use our brain? Could it be that we are born with an internal instruction manual? Might it be hidden inside each of us from birth? Within a language that many people overlook?

Welcome to Smartview Stories™ - a children's self-empowerment book project! Our emotional literacy stories help unlock this instruction manual and its hidden language. Our body and brain are always wanting our well-being. We can learn their language. This language reveals what is going on inside of us and around us. With practice, a mutual trust develops within us. What did not seem at all possible IS possible.

Our setting is Smartview Village. We base it on a lovely Appalachian tourist spot called Smart View Recreation Area along the Blue Ridge Parkway near Floyd, VA, USA. We invite you to visit this Recreation Area some time to experience for yourself the land we write about. This is public land. No one lives here right now.

There are communities similar to Smartview Village in the Floyd area. If you visit Smart View Recreation Area, you will understand what a magical place this would be to deepen your relationship with yourself, with others, with nature and with all the world.

Our stories begin in 2018 when a group of people gather at the local library to find a way forward. All around them, they are experiencing cultural norms falling apart. It confuses them. Changing their habits is not easy. Changing their beliefs seems even harder. What is clear is that they can help each other. Staying together as a community brings a sense of safety. They can lean on each other.

Four colorful families commit that day to create a fun and safe place to improve their skills at navigating life situations of all kinds. One family offers to share the land they live on. Within a year, the other three families build small homes on this land. They come with jobs, hobbies and pets. All share skills they have learned. Somehow, they do things slower yet, get more done. Families pause a lot to help each other. Each person practices listening to their own inner knowing. They practice listening to nature and the world around them. The way they live changes. These families recognize the value of sharing their stories.

From the greatest joys to the deepest shames, our characters practice the power of the pause. In that pause, they listen within themselves. Turning within becomes a fascinating journey as they learn to read this unfamiliar language. Neuroscience tells us that our brains are more complex than the entire universe yet discovered. It is with this understanding that our journey begins. What a ride this will be!

You can visit Smart View Recreational Area Virginia, USA

Elevation: 2503 ft.

The name Smart View refers to the long range, peaceful and colorful views here.

This recreation area includes picnic grounds, restrooms, hiking trails and the Trail Cabin exhibit. The exhibit is a one room dwelling built in the early 1890s and moved here.

The land is a mix of moist woodland, hardwood forest and open fields. Stones and rocks are abundant. There are several streams and one marshy area.

Smart View is a welcoming home for birds and wildlife.

Smartview Village Map

Smartview Village Family Trees

Grampy grew up on this property. It is magical. When Grammy joined him, he took her first to the grove of old oak trees. The pair walk here daily and came to know these trees as family. When Grampy welcomed other families to live here, he invited them to walk the property, listen to the land and commit to join a family of trees here. Our map shows the tree each family chose and where they built their home. Symbols under the tree remind us of ways this family bonds with each other.

When you visit Smartview Recreation Area, an old log cabin is on the same site as the **Oak** Family tree on our map. Grampy & Grammy's home is much larger. It resembles farm homes you'll see along the Blue Ridge Parkway. It is white with wide covered porches. They often host Sunday brunch and music jams on their porch. Grammy picks baskets of food from the gardens for Grampy to cook with. When they are not hosting friends, they often visit them on Grampy's motorcycle.

Large lemon petals from Poplar Tree flowers were covering the ground the day Sam, Dawn, Stryder and Wendy came to Smartview to choose their tree. The girls collected the petals. The guys pointed out how fast, straight and tall it grows. With this tree's majesty plus artistic leaves and petals, the **Poplar** tree felt like a match for this family. Shared time revolves around the arts and the outdoors. They all use bikes to get around. Someone from the family often joins Mama Dawn when she canoes on nearby Falls Lake.

Doug is a master woodworker, and his favorite wood is maple. Mina, Terri and Lynette knew before they came to walk that their family tree would be **Maple**. They found plenty to fall in love with. The girls danced in circles, twisting and turning playfully like maple seeds falling to the ground. Terri challenged her family to walk across a maple that had fallen over a stream. Mina sang a poem about the beauty of red-orange-yellow maple leaves. This family shares a love for nature and wildlife. They invite birds in close to their home. They like to look for and create special spaces to meditate in nature at Smartview.

As a newly blended family, Aunt Betty, Amber and Perla took several visits to choose their tree. They hugged this tree and that. Aunt Betty's favorite childhood dresser, her oldest piece of furniture, is cherry wood. Dangling white blossoms cover the black cherry trees in late spring. Their fruit feeds a wide variety of birds and other wildlife. Perla pointed out cherries go with good things like ice cream sundaes, and they all cheered 'Yes'! The **Cherry** Family plays a board game to relax after dinner. They all enjoy cooling off with a swim at the pond on hot summer days.

Prologue

It's story time, my Companions! Let's gather around.

Ashamaya fluffs its wings out to each side. Hummah takes a seat on one side. Sleuthin follows. The owl waits as they settle in.

Ashamaya smiles and then speaks. "It is time to help Smartview Village tell another set of Focusing stories. Our mission for this book involves awkward moments. I wonder what comes for each of you when you hear the phrase 'Awkward Moments'.

Sleuthin starts. "Ugh. Clumsy. Difficult. Unmanageable. No skill. Very annoying."

The owl nods. "Yes, I hear this phrase brings up a lot that can annoy you."

Hummah chimes in, "For me, awkward brings an image of tripping over my own arms or tying them in knots. It's downright embarrassing and might even be painful."

Ashamaya's face softens as it imagines this experience. "Oh, my! And for you, awkward moments bring a sense of embarrassment, maybe even pain. Thank you for sharing. This is a splendid start. And, there is more I'd like you to watch for as we help our friend Wendy. Our story involves Wendy at her new school."

Hummah is quiet. Sleuthin rolls his eyes and says, "I am not surprised."

Ashamaya smiles. "Mmm, this is helpful, Sleuthin. Surprise is a word I wanted to bring up. Are awkward moments planned or more of a surprise?"

Both Hummah and Sleuthin's eyes widen. Sleuthin says, "Well, you know I only like surprises I plan."

The owl smiles and nods. "Yes, I understand this about you, Sleuthin."

Hummah says, "I get this. Awkward moments would often be unexpected. I will want to help Wendy slow down her breath. I imagine she could go into fight or flight or freeze if it's not a joyful surprise."

Sleuthin sighs. "I could bring in memories that help. Seems risky. Is there another way I can help?"

"Ah, Sleuthin, you know a lot that can help Wendy," replies the owl. "What is something she likes to 'do' that helps her process her problems?"

"Oh yes! I can encourage her to draw! That will be easy!" says Sleuthin, more excited now that he has a clear job assignment.

Hummah waves an arm. "I will support you, Sleuthin. Show her the idea and I'll add colors. I will remind her how calming it feels to create with her hands."

Sleuthin and Hummah give each other a high-five as they shout, "together as a team!"

They both look up at Ashamaya, "Anything more?" asks Sleuthin. "Are we ready?" asks Hummah.

"Together as a team feels great. Thank you both so much for this," says the owl. "Yes, we are ready. A lusciously ripe time to adventure!"

A Puddly Kind of Day

Wendy holds her head high as she steps off the school bus. She hears kids snicker as the bus pulls away.

As soon as it rounds the corner, she bursts into tears and begins running wildly home.

As she sobs, she hears all sorts of thoughts flying through her mind.

'This was the worst day!'

'How did this happen?!'

'Let's not go back there!'

As she sees her house, she slows down to a walk and her sobs became sniffles.

When we feel bad, Ashamaya has many ways to help us find our way to feeling better.

Moving slower now, she takes in the bigger scene to her left. A favorite field, the sky,

One way to feel better is to pause and look around us. Find something to look at that feels comforting.

the trees, and the sound of birds welcome her home.

Wendy would see something like this on her left as she walked home. A 2019 picture from the real Smart View Recreation Area.

Wendy remembers her Papa's words "If ever the world does not

> Deep breaths that go into our belly show our body we are safe and can relax.

seem right, come home to your breath." She puts her hand on her belly to check she is breathing deep. Ah, yes, deep breaths.

"Oh, what do I do now?" Wendy wonders. She sees an image of her crayons.

A bit of a smile touches the corners of her mouth. As Wendy enters the kitchen, she goes straight to the cabinet. She pulls out a large box of crayons and some paper. She sits down at the kitchen table.

Ashamaya helps us listen within ourselves to more than just words.

Wendy sits still for a while, listening within herself. Then she begins to draw.

"Hello, Wendy." says Mama as she enters the kitchen. "Ahh... I see you are drawing. I wonder if this is about your day."

At the sound of Mama's voice, tears rolled down Wendy's cheeks. "Yes, Mama, something in me is sad and confused about school today."

Mama gently kisses the top of Wendy's head. "Oh, yes, I hear the sadness. And, oh my, tears are here, too." She looks at Wendy's drawing. "It looks like you are deep in process. Remember, sweetie, I am here if you want to talk about what happened. And, telling me may feel like going backward in your process. Listen to your body in deciding."

Wendy nods. "Thanks, Mama. I would rather not tell you now. This wants my attention. I will tell you another time, after I feel better."

Wendy looks down at her picture.

She tilts her head to one side.

And then to the other.

"Mama," Wendy says, "there is something more coming too."

Many of us listen only to thoughts we hear and miss our body wisdom. Our body has a language of its own that takes practice to "hear".

"Oh good," says Mama. "You might imagine Ashamaya is here, helping you create space for more understanding. I will make us a snack."

Mama makes a snack of bread, cheese, and sliced tomatoes.

Stryder bounds into the kitchen. "Do I smell snacks?"

Mama laughs. "Oh, yes, what a skilled nose you have!" She brings the tray to the table.

As Stryder looks toward Wendy, Mama says, "Wendy is drawing about her hard day. She is listening for something more that is coming."

Stryder nods. "Ok. I would like to help. I will shift my energy and hang out for a bit."

Stryder is very active. His body is always moving. He knows he will need Hummah helping him slow down here. Notice how he moves his attention from his mind to his body over the next few minutes.

Slowly, he lifts his right leg up to his chest.

He breathes in and out.

Then gradually, Stryder stretches his right leg out straight in front of him.

And ever so gently, Stryder puts his leg down.

He has moved forward a huge step!

Stryder glances toward Wendy to see if she is watching.

She is. A smile passes across her face.

Now Stryder does this same careful movement with his left leg. He brings his left leg up high, close to his chest.

He takes two breaths here.

Stryder knows he can help his sister see her situation from the eyes of Ashamaya by doing his slowing down in a fun way.
Do you ever use gentle humor like this to help someone around you smile and feel better?

Now slowly, and gently, he extends his left leg out straight in front of him.

He brings his foot, ever so gradually, down to the floor in front of him.

I wonder if you could take steps this slowly? Want to try it now? Is it hard for you?

He has traveled across the kitchen in just two giant steps!

Wendy lets out a giggle.

Calmly, Stryder sits down in the chair across from Wendy.

He is eager to listen.

When Wendy's eyes meet Stryder's eyes, Stryder says, "Where are you with your process so far?"

Wendy groans. Tears form in the corners of her eyes.

Closing her eyes, she explains, "I did not see it coming! What a surprise! I heard a voice. When I turned around, a large group of kids were watching me. As they laughed, it felt like a slow-motion wave of cold, icy water splashed over me. I stood there alone, kind of frozen."

Wendy pauses with this feeling for a minute; her eyes closed. Shivers move through her body.

You might pause here too. Can you remember being surprised? Sometimes surprises are fun. Sometimes they are not. Which kind is this?

Slow-motion means that it felt to Wendy like time slowed down. Hummah is the part of us that understands time can do this, feel fast or feel slow. Sleuthin likes to use a clock for time. The laughter may have only lasted 10 seconds on a clock. Here, Wendy is aware of how Hummah, her body, felt about the time.

"Now," Wendy says, "I feel this as part of me, kind of like a tree in a bad rainstorm. She cannot move, all wet and shivery."

Wendy's eyes open wide. "Oh, and then the bell rang."

Mama and Stryder nod listening.

Holding up her left arm, Wendy gestures to the left. "Over here, these kids move away laughing and joking like they had just won some kind of game!"

"Ahh, the kids on your left acted like they won," Mama says, "I'm wondering where they are in this picture of your space."

Wendy pauses with her eyes closed. More shivers go through her body. "I hear them now as something being mean and blaming me. Like it is my fault they had to be mean." Wendy sighs.

Mama says, "You might invite Ashamaya to help you here again. It sounds like these thoughts need to be in the distance a bit to keep your inner space safe."

Stepping back from our feelings and judgments is a skill Ashamaya helps us with. They can be here and we do not need to react or act from them. We are bigger.

"For sure Mama," says Wendy, "They are not being nice right now. They feel like crows up on a wire, cawing and cawing loudly at the tree. I will add them."

Wendy picks up her crayons. As she draws the crows, tears stream down her cheeks.

Stryder says softly, "Oh, now, here come tears."

Wendy nods, crying and smiling at the same time. She holds up her right arm with a loud, frustrated sigh. "Over here, on my right, was this awful, awkward silence. In some strange way, the silence comes with sadness and tears."

Mama softens her voice. "Whoa… let's pause here. You might take that idea of 'awful, awkward silence' back inside. See if those words fit with the sadness and tears."

Wendy and Stryder both raise their eyebrows. They nod at each other, taking in this new point.

Sleuthin helps us check details like this.

Wendy draws something more
and holds up her picture for
them to see.

"Oh, this really helps Mama," Wendy says. "I feel like everything is here now. My body is the bare tree, getting soaked in a cold rain, unable to move. The crows are laughing. This dog is the kids who watched in silence. The dog feels sad and awkward that there is a conflict."

"Nice," says Stryder. "I see each of those in your picture. Altogether in the same space."

Wendy nods. "Yep."

Wendy's eyes glance toward the snack tray. She reaches for some and then passes the tray to Stryder.

They all eat together in silence.

Mama and Stryder wait patiently for Wendy to speak next.

Ashamaya creating space.

As they finish their snacks, Wendy breaks the silence with a sigh… "

Something in me is still standing there soppy. It feels awkward. How can I ever go back to school after this?"

Stryder stands up to act out her mood. He softens his knees

and sways from side to side. His whole body moves gently, like a young tree.

"Like this, yes?" he says.

Wendy nods.

Now Stryder moves more loosely, like a wet noodle. Soon, his feet move a little.

Stryder suggests, "Maybe it feels kinda like this, shuffling its feet in a muddy puddle."

Wendy pauses, listening within herself.

"YES!" Wendy punches both arms above her in the air. "It's so PUDDLY standing in that mess! What a perfect image!"

Hummah exploring puddly within Stryder.

She stands up tall. "I get it! It wants me to be ok to BE ME when I go back to school!"

Wendy pauses. "No wonder some kids laughed and some were silent. I did something they did not understand."

Wendy stands next to Stryder. They both move their bodies like wet noodles, shuffling their feet in a puddle.

Mama joins them with her own body shuffle. "Oh, what a great way to deal with an awkward moment!"

When something shifts to a more positive feeling within us, it is important to pause and invite this new better feeling to be here as much as it would like. This is our new understanding of the situation. Stryder and Mama understand this and join in to support Wendy.
If they walked away now her process could easily slip backward. Stryder has a great idea...

"Hey, Wendy, I ran by a huge puddle over by the barn. Would you like to check it out?" says Stryder.

"For sure!" says Wendy.

Wendy skips happily down the drive.

Stryder runs alongside her.

They play in the puddle, splashing the muddy water all around.

The sun shines on them.

It's not long before the puddle
is dry.

The Bus Ride

Wendy's first few minutes on the bus were normal. Perfectly normal.

She got on the bus and sat down next to her best friend Tamara. They always sat together. Wendy spent a few minutes looking around and getting settled.

Hmmm. Something is off.

You might remember a time your body told you, "Something is off. " How did it get your attention? This is Hummah's power. She is always sensing our environment.

Wendy notices how quiet Tamara is. Tamara is looking out the window. This is not normal.

Wendy tilts her head forward smiling. "Good morning Tamara."

Tamara turns her face toward Wendy. Whoa, Wendy thinks, she looks awful. Her face is tight, like she is in pain.

As their eyes meet, tears roll down Tamara's cheeks. "Oh Wendy, I am so sick.

My tummy. I wish I had stayed home. What if I throw up before we get to school?"

Wendy's mind flashes an image. It was from this summer when she got carsick. Her mom had given her a bag to hold. The bag had saved her from making a big mess. Where could she find one?

Wendy feels a panic rising as she imagines them both sprayed with puke.

Hummah shows Wendy here what she is most afraid of. No wonder!

Wendy feels herself pause.

This would be a good time for Ashamaya to help this worry feel seen.

She takes a deep breath to meet the panic rising in her chest.

Slowly, her breath releases.

She becomes curious. Maybe she has something like a bag?

 Wendy remembered the plastic pouch of colored pencils she had in her backpack. She unzips her backpack. Wendy dumps the pencils in there. She places the plastic pouch in Tamara's hand and whispers. "Here, in case you need it!"

Tamara smiles weakly back at her.

Wendy says, "Let's breathe together. Get your belly the air it needs to do the best it can." Each places a hand on their lower belly. They follow their breath inward all the way, feeling their hand move.

As she sat there, Wendy's mind raced into the past. She chose public school this year to spend more time with Tamara. They were best friends. Tamara told her such fun stories about lunch, recess, music, and art classes.

Listening to Tamara's stories, Wendy would dream about sharing fun school times together.

If she went to Turtle Spring with Stryder, she would not know anyone in her class.

So here she was, happy to be helping her sick friend.

Wendy looks over at Tamara. "Remember, I'm here." Tamara nods.

Wendy brings her awareness back inside. Something new is forming.

Something that is uncomfortable about school. It started as a little doubt. This doubt worried other kids would not like her. Now that some kids had teased her, it was hard not to agree with.

The doubt-worry gets so strong, Wendy starts to feel sick herself. Oh, dear. She puts both hands on her belly. Silently, she responds to her belly, "Oh my, I hear you, so very much worry."

A minute passes. Wendy's belly seems better. Suddenly, in a glimpse, she catches an understanding.

Ahhh…

Something in me is afraid Tamara will go home sick. Oh, no wonder.

Ashamaya is helping Wendy listen gently to her doubt-worry. Whenever we have a doubt-worry come to our attention, we can practice these focusing skills.

1. Say hello to IT.
   Let IT know you see it.
2. Notice if IT feels big or little.
3. Tell IT what you think it wants you to understand.
4. Check back with IT.
   Yes? No? Maybe?
   Do you understand it right?

When the bus arrives at school, Wendy walks with Tamara right to the school office. The school nurse will call her parents. They will come and take her home.

Wendy walks to her classroom. She seems ok for morning homeroom. As she becomes busy with morning classes, the upset in her belly starts getting stronger. Ugh. It feels like a churning. Up and down, round and round. Over and over. She wishes the upset would leave her alone. Geez, she feels worse than getting off a crazy roller coaster ride.

Didn't IT understand she was nervous enough since Tamara had gone home sick?

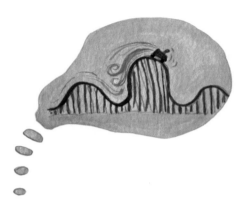

Wendy's belly churning up and down…

Wendy's stomach slowed down only when she focused on taking slow breaths deep into her belly.

It is often helpful to breath toward pain or discomfort in our body. Something in us that does not like pain sometimes directs air flow away from here. It thinks it is helping us ignore the pain. Instead, without air flow, this discomfort in our body is often forced to get stronger.

At lunch, Wendy eats two bites of her sandwich and gives up. Too much belly churning to eat food.

Uh - oh.

This is when she realized her amygdala had taken over.

Ugh. The doubt-worry had gotten so big, her body was stressed. It believes she needs protection. No wonder she sat at the noisiest table. Her amygdala protector is hiding her in the noise. It worked too. No one was paying any attention to her. "Good job," Wendy says to herself. "And I am ok."

A whopper sigh comes out.
Whew. Yes, she is ok.

Wendy spends the rest of lunch looking at the colorful painting on the wall. There were trees, birds, and kids playing. This helps her feel a little calmer.

Our amygdala is a part of our brain. It is small and has two parts. One part thinks like Hummah and the other thinks like Sleuthin. Both act to protect us. They are always watching out for our safety.

If either one thinks we are in danger, we will become anxious or stressed. One way to help our amygdala relax is to look around us. Notice normal cheerful things. Maybe you are wearing your favorite shoes or the sun is shining outside. This shows our amygdala we are really ok. We are not in danger.

Without Tamara, Wendy has no interest in recess outside. She asks her teacher if she can stay indoors to draw. Yes. Yay!

Wendy brings colored pencils and paper over to a chair in the sun. For 5 minutes, she stares at her paper. Then, with the brown pencil, she begins drawing in the bottom center of the page. This becomes the churning in her belly. She adds black and red.

Drawing helps Wendy listen. She senses fear in her churning belly. Ah, the churning is afraid of being alone. No wonder. Wendy senses guilt here too. Something in her afraid-of-being-alone wanted to go to this school. Now it doubts that choice. Maybe being-alone at home is easier than being-alone at school. Ah, yes, she understands what it means.

Now the guilt becomes more like surprise. Oh, yea, going to this school had brought surprises. She writes the word 'Surprise!' in the center of her paper. It feels like it needs some love, so she draws a heart around it. She sits still again, listening inside her body.

Memories flash into her head of the day she froze as kids teased and laughed at her. Her nose gets a whiff of diesel smell. Ahh. Something in her is worried that may happen again on the bus. Oh, that is possible! For the first time, Tamara, her seat buddy, is sick.

Oh, wait, those same kids who tease her are not on her bus. She welcomes that. A wave of relief moves through her.

The word 'puddly' comes too.
Oh yes. She smiled about
Stryder helping her find her
own sense of puddly. She
writes the word puddly on top
of her paper. She fills the top
and edges with cheerful curly
marks. With each color she
adds, she feels more confident
that the bus ride home will be
ok.

The rest of the afternoon sped by for Wendy. Before she knew it, she was getting on the bus. She decided that IF her regular seat was open; she would sit there. Why not? Most likely, no one would sit with her.

She sits down in their usual spot. Putting her backpack on the seat, she takes up over half the seat. Whew!

Wendy lets out a big sigh.

The backpack will help keep her safe. She looks out the window and imagines being home soon.

The bus driver puts the bus in gear. Wendy smiles to herself. The seat next to her is empty.

Wait! Suddenly, her eyebrows shoot upward. Someone is squeezing into the spot next to her. She first sees their feet. Then a backpack appears on the floor between their feet. Who is this?

"Hi, my name is Harrison. Is it ok if I sit with you today?" he says.

"Uh, sure." Wendy moves her backpack to the floor. She scoots over a bit.

Her sense is that Harrison wants to be friendly. She takes a deep breath and lets the air out slow. Then she hears Harrison do the same. Interesting. He must be nervous to sit by her. He is so big he must be a 5th grader. Why would a 5th grader be nervous? Wendy becomes curious. In a flash, she realizes she had not told him her name.

Wendy turns toward Harrison and says, "My name is Wendy."

He smiles and nods.

Wendy looks confused.

Lowering his voice, he says, "I help in the office. I saw you there the other day."

Wendy had forgotten all about being in the front office. Oh my goodness! Now, a flood of memories reminds her.

Harrison leans forward, as if telling her a secret. He pauses and meets her gaze. She leans in toward him and perks up her left ear.

"I talk to plants too," he whispers.

'Whoa…' Wendy thinks silently to herself, 'have I just made a new friend?'

Harrison smiles at Wendy. Her eyes tell him she understands.

 "I can help you with the plants if you like," Harrison says.

Wendy lets this new idea in. "Yes, it would be fun to have a plant friend."

"Cool," says Harrison. "I'll be helping in the office on Friday. I can introduce you to the office plants then."

Harrison looks up toward the front of the bus. "This is my stop." He nods toward her as he gets off the bus. "See ya, Wendy."

Wendy closes her eyes and gives herself a hug. Wow. There was nothing routine about riding the bus today!

Ashamaya helping Wendy hug herself.

Glimmers of Bloom

Wendy skips home when she gets off the bus. She wants to tell her family this whole thing about school. It seems best to wait until dinner.

She plays in the woods until she hears the dinner bell ring. Once they start eating, Wendy begins wiggling noisily in her chair.

Mama, Papa and Stryder pause their eating to look her way. Mama leans toward 4-year-old Levi sitting near her. Mama catches his gaze and moves her eyes toward Wendy. Little Levi follows her gaze. Even their dog Casey notices and tilts his head with curiosity toward Wendy.

Wendy sits up tall in her chair. "A lot happened to me at school this week that goes with my puddly situation."

Papa nods, meeting her eyes. "Ah. A lot happened. If it feels right to share now, we'd love to hear more."

Wendy begins slowly. "Well, did I tell you the kids were teasing me because I talk to the plants at school?"

They all shake their heads no.

Wendy sighs. "The plants at school are not healthy. I cannot ignore them. I greet them in the halls as I arrive at school. They are so glad to have my attention!"

"Ahh… yes," says Papa, nodding along with the others. "Plants appreciate you."

"Yes, the plants do. The kids, not so much Papa," Wendy says. "Some kids are uncomfortable and say silly or mean things. When I hear them, I look over their way. I nod to let them know I see them."

"Wow," says Stryder, "How brave! You are OK with being yourself!"

Wendy shivers, remembering. Then she beams a big smile. She gives herself a hug by crossing her arms across her chest.

Mama chimes in "Wendy, look, Levi understands."

They all look toward Levi. His eyes are big. A few tears run down his face. A smile rounds his cheeks. All at the same time.

Wendy says, "Oh, Levi, you get it! Being brave when other people do not understand you is hard."

Wendy hands Levi one of his stuffed birds. She gives herself another hug. "Can you hug yourself too, Levi? Red bird will help you. We are so glad you are here with us."

Levi hugs himself while holding his red bird.

The whole family stops eating to hug themselves.

"Yes," says Papa smiling, "We are so glad you are here with us Levi."

Papa picks up his fork. The family follows.

Hummah helps us enjoy tasting food.

As they are finishing their meal, Papa invites Wendy to continue her story.

"Yes," says Wendy, "I have been nodding toward the teasers for two weeks. I just give them a quick glance, or I can feel myself start to freeze like the first time. Some days are easier than others."

Wendy pauses. "Papa, do you think it is harder not to react when the teasers are standing closer?"

Papa brings his attention inside himself to listen. Nodding, he replies, "Oh, yes. Closer makes our amygdala more nervous that they might do more than tease."

Papa pushes back his chair. "I can explore this within myself. Let's imagine this hand is teasing my head. My hand is saying 'You are so weird!' I feel better when I hold my hand out here. As I move my hand closer, my neck tenses. My head pulls back. We could all try it."

Everyone puts their hand out and explores what Papa is doing.

"Yes, I get this, Papa," says Wendy. "It is harder when my teaser hands are close! I also must be nervous about looking at the kids for very long. I meet their eyes for a bit, then I look away. Something in me believes the teasers will experience a longer glance from me as threatening. It is protecting me."

Papa smiles. "I am impressed Wendy. There is wisdom here beyond your years. Yes, something is protecting you. In addition, I hear your ability to hold empathy for the entire situation. You do not need to risk threatening the other kids to feel ok about yourself. I learn so much from you Wendy."

Ashamaya being with something in Wendy that believes glancing at her teasers is safer.

Mama nods. "We all do."

Wendy takes this in. "Thank you. Something more I want to share is that I have two new friends at school. These friends like plants too."

Mama raises her eyebrows. Papa leans forward in his chair.

Wendy continues, "One friend is Mrs. Hoffar in the front office. She noticed that the plants I talk to are happier. She invited me to visit all the office and hallway plants any morning before the school bell rings. I can water and feed them. She is hoping I have ideas on moving them to better spots. Many plants are very sad now."

Wendy pauses. Her eyes light up as she looks at her family. "Lucky me!"

"Wow, Wendy, this is great for you and the school!" says Mama, "You know a lot about plants."

Wendy laughs. "Yes, and I will learn a lot more! She said there are 36 plants. I will get a tour of them all Friday morning. Some rooms have windows, some do not."

"Something more happened today. Harrison, an older boy from school, sat with me today on the way home. Tamara was sick. All day, I was so worried someone mean would sit next to me."

Wendy pauses and shakes her head. "Instead, I made a new friend. He whispered to me so no one else could hear. Guess what? Harrison talks to plants too! He offered to help me with the plants. I will not be alone now!"

'Not alone is precious.'

Wendy closes her eyes. "I closed my eyes when he got off the bus. It was a very special moment, like a dream come true to hear his words. I am really not alone. Not alone is precious."

In unison, Papa & Mama reflect "Ahh, not alone is precious."

Papa pushes back his chair. "Your choice to attend public school this year is giving you lots to process. I am so happy you are finding your way. This practice builds your awareness skills for life."

Mama has an idea. "Maybe this is something you'd like to draw or write about. A dream come true."

"Oh, I will do that, Mama!" says Wendy. "I can already tell there will be beautiful colors blending together."

'A Dream Come True' by Wendy

Appendix

Focusing

The relational skills our story characters practice is called Focusing. Focusing helps us pause for a moment and create space for new and unexpected possibilities. These skills are accessible to everyone and are improved over time with practice. The International Focusing Institute supports individuals and groups in developing these skills. For more information, check out www.focusing.org

Felt Sense Literacy

"We all agree that Focusing is a natural process. It is a capacity of every human being. Making an analogy with reading and writing, focusing is something everyone should be enabled to discover and develop. To view it along the lines of "literacy" places Focusing at the most basic level. It is something everyone can naturally have."
Marion Hendricks-Gendlin, Ph.D.
Felt Sense Literacy: focusing.org/literacy

Neuroscience

Neuroscience is the study of our nervous system. Our nervous system is more complex than the entire universe yet discovered. It is involved in every aspect of our body. Our behaviors, how we feel to what we know, plus our bodily activities, how we breath or move, are managed by our nervous system. Our nervous system has a lot of responsibility for our well-being.

Focusing gives us the skills to understand the language of our nervous system. Body sensations, emotions, moods, images, words, gestures and movements are all ways our body speaks to us every day. A yawn is our body communicating. A thought is our mind communicating. Our body does not lie if we learn how to check back to see if we are understanding it correctly.

We can make better choices when we understand how to access our deepest wisdom. We improve our relationship with ourselves by pausing to listen within.

Meet Our Inner Companions!

These three aspects of being human help us experience and live our life. They are with us in every moment. As we become more aware of them, we understand HOW to better support ourselves in all types of life situations. May this trio of inner companions inspire you in your journey toward thriving.

Hummah! [HUMM-ahh] This female companion is always monitoring our environment for us. She gives us access to all of our body senses: vision, sound, taste, smell, intuition (gut sense), touch and overall body wisdom. Hummah is fluid and flexible, a skilled shape-shifter. She is comfortable in the dark and okay with the unknown.

She is capable of broad, sustained alertness in ways of "being". Hummah says "I am your body". She helps us explore, create, connect and relate with the world. In fact, Hummah is so wired to connect that it can be hard for her to say no. Dance, art, music, nature and metaphor are some of her favorite activities. She is content to pursue these passionately with no sense of purpose. Hummah enjoys reading people's eyes. She often can tell how real someone's words are this way.

BEING is a way to remember Hummah.

Sleuthin! [Slu-THINN] This male companion helps us access all that we have learned about being a human on this planet. He loves to separate and label things, solve problems and find missing pieces. He is always engaged in some purpose, enjoys helping others and is efficient in routine situations.

Sleuthin prefers and defends what he knows! He is so happy when things are under control! Sometimes he worries about the future. And boy, does Sleuthin like to talk! He has access to our language center and can fire off endless repetitive thoughts when he does not feel heard.

Sleuthin says "I have a body" and has lots of ideas to keep it busy.

DOING is a way to remember Sleuthin.

Ashamaya! [AH-sha-my-ya] Through the power of the Pause, this unisex companion helps us claim our human birthright powers as wizards of love, time and space. The emphasis here is on process, we are forever in flux. Change ruffles no feathers here! Embodying trust, anything is possible.

Ashamaya understands that everything belongs. Everything. The owl's eye takes in an expansive mountain ridge view while its wings open wide to hold whatever is here right now with tenderness. No worry or fear is too big for the wings of Ashamaya. This creature can hold the entire planet when needed. It is the quality of the space that Ashamaya creates that sets a tone of cooperation, teamwork and trust in life's forward flow. We are in this together; the owl reminds us again and again. When we pause, open our wings with both kindness and clarity, we allow ourselves to grow toward our highest potential.

BEING WITH reminds us of Ashamaya.

A Peek at the Poplar Family!

Together, they enjoy biking, camping, art, singing and music. Mama Dawn and Papa Sam learned Focusing shortly before Stryder was born so that they could raise their kids with these skills. They are a typical busy family and feel blessed to be living Focusing as a way of life in community with others.

Age 38
Mama Dawn is a social butterfly, involved in helping others in the community. She works as an artisan potter. Her hobbies are gardening, Qi-gong, canoeing and biking.

Age 37
Papa Sam is the founder of a local nonprofit business dedicated to raising awareness about mindfulness skills. His hobbies are walking with Casey, his dog, video games and playing fiddle at Friday night jams in Floyd.

Age 11

Stryder likes to move and runs, bikes or plays basketball most every day. One of his goals is to join a local track team. Stryder feels movement helps him be more attentive when he is sitting to read or play a video game.

Age 8

Wendy is adaptable and likes to keep her options open. She loves to draw and is already a talented artist. Since moving here, her new hobby is plants, learning about them and spending time learning to communicate with them.

Age 4

Levi does not talk much. He is often sensitive, showing off one moment and closing down the next. Levi is Mama Dawn's nephew who recently joined the family. It's not clear how long he will be here. His parents live in a big city and travel often for their jobs. They hope Levi will thrive more in this environment. He loves birds and imitates bird sounds beautifully.

Age 3

Casey lives in adoration of her family. She is quite attentive to Papa Sam for walks, one-one time and treats. She is also quite happy that Levi is here. She often sits near him as he plays in a sunny rock patch outside the home.

Introducing our Smartview Stories Team!

Sandy & Inge at Smartview Recreation Area

Sandy Jahmi Burg, certified Focusing trainer with The International Focusing Institute, is the primary author and coordinator of this project. You might guess she is a neuroscience geek! Sandy has experience in permaculture design and has lived in small intentional communities since 2005.

Inge Terrill is a Focuser, educator, editor, wellness coach, biologist, and co-creator extraordinaire here. Inge is most familiar with the land where Smartview Stories take place. This was a favorite nature spot of her family's as her two daughters were growing up.

Our Illustrators!

Molly Gutiérrez lives with her husband, Sam, and their house full of fur babies in Roanoke, VA. She enjoys whipping up yummy things in the kitchen, digging in the dirt, healing through mind and body modalities, and discovering new depths through drawing.

Nomi Miller is a believer in magic and the power of words. She likes to draw, dance, sing, be silly and do nothing at all. She lives in a garden colony in Denmark with her baby-to-be.

Sarah Hall is a high school student in Floyd. She loves the arts — music, performing arts and especially, drawing. A psychology geek, Sarah enjoys learning how the brain works. She is parent to sixteen plants, and a friend to her dog, two cats and two hens.

Renee La Roi is an American Canadian, and a long time Focuser. She is also a certified Focusing professional, graphic artist and yogi. She loves to travel & bike & practice yoga outside --- she is a big dreamer.

Smartview Stories™ would not be where they are without all of the love the Smartview team breathes into this project!